VIKING CANADA

DAVE COOKS THE TURKEY

Master storyteller and humorist STUART MCLEAN writes and hosts the popular CBC Radio show *The Vinyl Cafe*. He is the author of the bestselling books *Vinyl Cafe Diaries*, which won the short fiction award from the Canadian Authors Association; *Home from the Vinyl Cafe* and *Vinyl Cafe Unplugged*, which both won the Stephen Leacock Award for Humour; and *Welcome Home: Travels in Smalltown Canada*, which won the CAA's award for non-fiction.

ALSO BY STUART McLEAN

The Morningside World of Stuart McLean

Welcome Home: Travels in Smalltown Canada

Stories from the Vinyl Cafe

Home from the Vinyl Cafe

Vinyl Cafe Unplugged

Vinyl Cafe Diaries

STUART McLEAN

DAVE

COOKS

THE

TURKEY

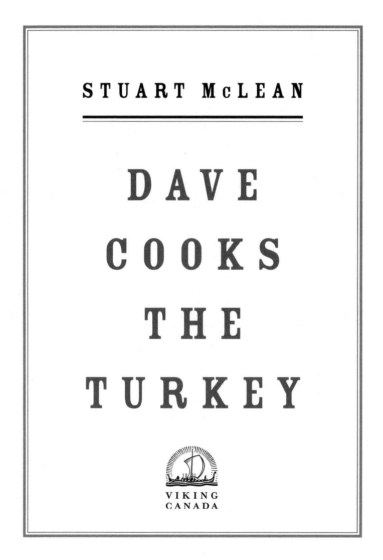

VIKING
CANADA

VIKING CANADA

Published by the Penguin Group

Penguin Group (Canada), 90 Eglinton Avenue East, Suite 700, Toronto, Ontario, Canada M4P 2Y3
  (a division of Pearson Penguin Canada Inc.)

Penguin Group (USA) Inc., 375 Hudson Street, New York, New York 10014, U.S.A.
Penguin Books Ltd, 80 Strand, London WC2R 0RL, England
Penguin Ireland, 25 St Stephen's Green, Dublin 2, Ireland (a division of Penguin Books Ltd)
Penguin Group (Australia), 250 Camberwell Road, Camberwell, Victoria 3124, Australia
  (a division of Pearson Australia Group Pty Ltd)
Penguin Books India Pvt Ltd, 11 Community Centre, Panchsheel Park, New Delhi – 110 017, India
Penguin Group (NZ), cnr Airborne and Rosedale Roads, Albany, Auckland 1310, New Zealand
  (a division of Pearson New Zealand Ltd)
Penguin Books (South Africa) (Pty) Ltd, 24 Sturdee Avenue, Rosebank, Johannesburg 2196, South Africa

Penguin Books Ltd, Registered Offices: 80 Strand, London WC2R 0RL, England

First published 2005

(FR) 10 9 8 7 6 5 4 3 2 1

Copyright © Stuart McLean, 2005
Illustrations © Wesley Bates, 2005

Designed by Paul Hodgson

Manufactured in Canada.

LIBRARY AND ARCHIVES CANADA CATALOGUING IN PUBLICATION

McLean, Stuart, 1948–
   Dave cooks the turkey / Stuart McLean.

ISBN 0-670-06445-9

I. Title.

PS8575.L448D38 2005   C813'.54   C2005-902815-7

Visit the Penguin Group (Canada) website at **www.penguin.ca**

Visit *The Vinyl Cafe* website at **www.cbc.ca/vinylcafe**

For anyone who has ever

entered a kitchen,

full of hope

T his is the first Christmas story I ever wrote for *The Vinyl Cafe*. And I had no idea when I was writing it that I was creating something of a Christmas tradition. Yet today, almost ten years later, when I run into people who want to talk to me about *The Vinyl Cafe* stories, I know someone will eventually bring up "Dave Cooks the Turkey"—usually to tell me it's their favourite of the Dave stories, sometimes to say they read it aloud every year at Christmas. Often to ask if it's true.

Well, yes, Virginia, there once was a turkey that was run around my neighbourhood from oven to oven, and, yes, it did spend some time in a hotel oven. But it was a *Thanksgiving* turkey, not a *Christmas* one. And it was my turkey, not Dave's. This was not long after I graduated from university, and my roommates and I threw an ill-advised Thanksgiving dinner. The bird, like the bird in the story, *was* grade B, and it *was* dubbed Butch, and it did get thawed at the last moment, though not with a hair dryer or an electric blanket.

Anyway, that was long ago and far away. The story has a life of its own now.

We play it on the radio show almost every year, so I don't read this story on stage any more. I do, however, remember a Vinyl Cafe concert a few years ago when I came close. For the first half of the show I was being distracted by a noise coming from the back of the theatre. It was, I finally figured out, a woman's voice, and it seemed, from my vantage point on stage, to be cackling.

"What are you *doing*?" I finally asked.

"Gobble, gobble, gobble," called the woman.

It finally dawned on me. The woman was requesting "The Turkey Story."

It's a disconcerting thing, to be gobbled at in public, even if it is meant as a compliment. I didn't read the turkey story that night, but if I'd had this little book, I might have given her a copy. I would have told her what many people tell me—that they like to read it out loud.

Nothing delights me more than the idea of people coming together around one of my stories to share in laughter. Especially during the dark nights of winter. I hope that you enjoy this version of "Dave Cooks the Turkey," whether read aloud with friends and family, or enjoyed on your own in the kind of quiet pre-Christmas calm that Morley and Dave can only dream about.

Stuart McLean

DAVE COOKS THE TURKEY

W hen Carl Lowbeer bought his wife, Gerta, *The Complete Christmas Planner,* he did not understand what he was doing. If Carl had known how much Gerta was going to enjoy the book, he would not have given it to her. He bought it on the afternoon of December 23. A glorious day. Carl left work at lunch and spent the afternoon drifting around downtown—window shopping, and listening to carollers and falling into conversations with complete strangers. When he stopped for coffee he was shocked to see it was 5:30. Shocked because the only things he had bought were a book by Len Deighton and some shaving cream in a tube—both things he planned to wrap and give himself. That's when the Joy of Christmas, who had sat down with him and bought him a double chocolate croissant, said, I think I'll stay here and have another coffee while you finish your shopping. The next thing Carl knew, he was ripping through the mall like a prison escapee.

On Christmas Eve, Carl found himself staring at a bag full of stuff he couldn't remember buying. He wondered if he might have picked up someone else's bag by mistake, but then he found a receipt with his signature on it. Why would he have paid twenty-three dollars for a slab of metal to defrost meat when they already owned a microwave oven that would do it in half the time? Who could he possibly have been thinking of when he bought the ThighMaster?

Carl did remember buying *The Complete Christmas Planner*. It was the picture on the cover that drew him to the book— a picture of a woman striding across a snow-covered lawn with a wreath of chili peppers tucked under her arm. The woman looked as if she was in a hurry, and that made Carl think of Gerta so he bought the book, never imagining that it was something that his wife had been waiting for all her life. Carl was as surprised as anyone last May when Gerta began the neighbourhood Christmas group. Although not, perhaps, as surprised as Dave was when his wife, Morley, joined it.

"**I**t's not about Christmas, Dave," said Morley. "It's about getting together."

The members of Gerta's group, all women, met every second Tuesday night, at a different house each time.

They drank tea, or beer, and the host baked something, and they worked on stuff. Usually until about eleven.

"But that's not the point," said Morley. "The *point* is getting together. It's about neighbourhood—not about what we are actually doing."

But there was no denying that they were doing stuff. Christmas stuff.

"It's wrapping paper," said Morley.

"You are *making* paper?" said Dave.

"*Decorating* paper," said Morley. "This is hand-printed paper. Do you know how much this would cost?"

That was in July.

In August they dipped oak leaves in gold paint and hung them in bunches from their kitchen ceilings to dry.

Then there was the stencilling weekend. The weekend Dave thought if he didn't keep moving, Morley would stencil him.

In September Dave couldn't find an eraser anywhere in the house, and Morley said, "That's because I took them all with me. We're making rubber stamps."

"You are *making* rubber stamps?" said Dave.

"Out of erasers," said Morley.

"People don't even *buy* rubber stamps any more," said Dave.

"This one is going to be an angel," said Morley, reaching into her bag. "I need a metallic ink stamp pad. Do you think you could buy me a metallic ink stamp pad and some more gold paint? And we need some of those snap things that go into Christmas crackers."

"The what things?" said Dave.

"The exploding things you pull," said Morley. "We are going to make Christmas crackers. Where do you think we could get the exploding things?"

There were oranges drying in the basement on the clothes rack and blocks of wax for candles stacked on the ping-pong table.

One day in October Morley said, "Do you know there are only sixty-seven shopping days until Christmas?"

Dave did not know this. In fact he had not completely unpacked from their summer vacation. Without thinking he said, "What are you talking about?"

And Morley said, "If we wanted to get all our shopping done by the week before Christmas we only have"—she shut her eyes—"sixty-two days left."

Dave and Morley usually *start* their shopping the week before Christmas.

And there they were, with only sixty-seven shopping days left, standing in their bedroom staring at each other, incomprehension hanging between them.

It hung there for a good ten seconds.

Then Dave said something he had been careful not to say for weeks. He said, "I thought this thing wasn't about Christmas."

He immediately regretted his words as Morley left the room. And then came back. Like a locomotive.

She said, "Don't make fun of me, Dave."

"Uh oh," thought Dave.

"What," said Morley

"I didn't say that," said Dave.

"You said 'uh oh,'" said Morley.

"I thought 'uh oh,'" said Dave. "I didn't *say* 'uh oh.' Thinking 'uh oh' isn't like saying 'uh oh.' They don't send you to jail for *thinking* you want to strangle someone."

"What?" said Morley.

Morley slept downstairs that night. She didn't say a word when Dave came down and tried to talk her out of it. Didn't say a word the next morning until Sam and Stephanie had left for school. Then she said, "Do you know what my life is like, Dave?"

Dave suspected—correctly—she wasn't looking for an answer.

"My life is a train," she said. "I am a train. Dragging everyone from one place to another. To school and to dance class and to now–it's–time–to–get–up and now–it's–time–to–go–to–bed. I'm a train full of people who complain when you try to get them into a bed and fight when you try to get them out of one. That's my job. And I'm not only the train, I'm the porter and the conductor and the cook and the engineer and the maintenance man. And I print the tickets and stack the luggage and clean the dishes. And if they still had cabooses, I'd be in the caboose."

Dave didn't want to ask where the train was heading. He had the sinking feeling that somewhere up ahead someone had pulled up a section of the track.

"And you know where the train is going, Dave?" said Morley.

Yup, he thought. Off the tracks. Any moment now.

"What?" said Morley.

"No," said Dave. "I don't know where the train's going."

Morley leaned over the table.

"The train chugs through the year, Dave. Through Valentine's Day and Easter and then summer holidays. Through a town called First Day of School and past the village of Hallowe'en and the township of Class Project, and down the spur line called Your Sister Is Visiting. And you know what's at the end of the track? You know where my train is heading?"

Dave looked around nervously. He didn't want to get this wrong. He would have been happy to say where the train was going if he knew he could get it right. Was his wife going to leave him? Maybe the train was going to D-I-V-O-R-C-E.

"Not at Christmas," he mumbled.

"Exactly," said Morley. "To the last stop on the line—Christmas dinner. And this is supposed to be something I look forward to, Dave. Christmas is supposed to be a heart-warming family occasion."

"Christmas dinner," said Dave tentatively. It seemed a reasonably safe thing to say.

Morley nodded.

Feeling encouraged Dave added, "With a turkey and stuffing and everything."

But Morley wasn't listening.

"And when we finally get through that week between Christmas and New Year, you know what they do with the train?"

Dave shook his head.

"They back it up during the night when I am asleep so they can run it through all the stations again."

Dave nodded earnestly.

"And you know who you are, Dave?"

Dave shook his head again. No. No, he didn't know who he was. He was hoping maybe he was the engineer. Maybe he was up in the locomotive. Busy with men's work.

Morley squinted at her husband.

"You are the guy in the bar car, Dave, pushing the button to ask for another drink."

By the way Morley said that, Dave could tell that she still loved him. She could have told him, for instance, that he had to get out of the bar car. Or, for that matter, off the train. She hadn't. Dave realized it had been close, and if he was going to stay aboard, he was going to have to join the crew.

The next weekend he said, "Why don't I do some of the Christmas shopping? Why don't you give me a list, and

I will get things for everyone in Cape Breton?"

Dave had never gone Christmas shopping in October. He was unloading bags onto the kitchen table when he said, "That wasn't so bad."

Morley walked across the kitchen and picked up a book that had fallen on the floor. "I'm sorry," she said. "It's just that I like Christmas so much. I *used* to like Christmas so much. I was thinking that if I got everything done early maybe I could enjoy it again. I'm trying to get control of it, Dave. I'm trying to make it fun again. That's what this is all about."

Dave said, "What else can I do?"

Morley reached out and touched his elbow and said, "On Christmas Day, after we have opened the presents, I want to take the kids to work at the food bank. I want you to look after the turkey."

"I can do that," said Dave.

D ave didn't understand the full meaning of what he had agreed to do until Christmas Eve, when the presents were finally wrapped and under the tree and he was snuggled, warm and safe, in bed. It was one of his favourite moments of the year. He nudged his wife's feet. She gasped.

"Did you take the turkey out of the freezer?" she said.

"Yes, of course," said Dave.

Of course he hadn't. But he wasn't about to admit that. He wasn't about to tell Morley he couldn't hold up his end of a bargain. So Dave lay in bed, his eyes closed, his body rigid, the minutes of the night dragging by as he monitored his wife's breathing.

Forty minutes went by before he dared open an eye. "Morley?" he said softly.

There was no answer.

Dave gingerly lifted her hand off his shoulder and when she didn't stir, rolled himself off the bed in slow motion, dropping like a shifty cartoon character onto the carpet beside Arthur the dog. A moment later he periscoped up to check if Morley was still sleeping and saw her hand patting the bed, searching for him. He picked it up, looked around desperately, and then shoved the confused dog onto the forbidden bed. He placed Morley's hand on Arthur's head, holding his breath as they both settled. Then he crawled out of the bedroom.

There was no turkey in the basement freezer. Dave peered into it in confusion. He lifted an open package of hot dogs. Then he dove his upper body into the freezer chest, his feet lifting off the ground as he rattled around inside, emerging a moment later empty handed and panicked. He ran upstairs and jerked open the freezer in the fridge. Bags of frozen vegetables tumbled out as he searched it frantically.

There was no turkey in the upstairs freezer either. Dave stood in front of the fridge as if he had been struck by a mallet—so stunned that he was able to watch but not react to the can of frozen orange-juice concentrate as it slowly rolled out of the open freezer and began a slow-motion freefall towards his foot. He watched it with the dispassionate curiosity of a scientist.

The metal edge of the orange-juice container landed on his big toe. Before he felt the pain shoot up his leg and settle exquisitely between his eyes, there was a moment of no pain, a moment when he was able to formulate a thought. The thought was, *This is going to hurt.* Then he was stuffing his fist into his mouth to stop himself from crying out.

That was the moment, the moment when he was hopping around the kitchen chewing on his fist, that Dave realized that looking after the turkey, something he had promised to do, meant *buying* it as well as putting it in the oven.

Dave unloaded both freezers to be sure. Then he paced around the kitchen trying to decide what to do. When he finally went upstairs, Morley was still asleep. He considered waking her. Instead, he lay down and imagined, in painful detail, the chronology of the Christmas Day waiting for him. Imagined everything from the first squeal of morning to that moment when his family came home from the food bank expecting a turkey dinner. He could see the dark look that would cloud his wife's face when he carried a bowl of pasta across the kitchen and placed it on the table she would have set with the homemade crackers and the gilded oak leaves.

He was still awake at 2:00 A.M., but at least he had a plan. He would wait until they left for the food bank. Then he would take off to some deserted Newfoundland outport and live under an assumed name. At Sam's graduation one of his friends would ask, "Why isn't your father here?" and Sam would explain that "one Christmas he forgot to buy the turkey and he had to leave."

At 3:00 A.M., after rolling around for an hour, Dave got out of bed, dressed, and made himself a big pot of coffee. He gulped down a large mugful and slipped quietly out the back door. He was looking for a twenty-four-hour grocery store. It was either that or wait for the food bank to open, and though he couldn't think of anyone in the city more in need of a turkey, the idea that his family might spot him in line made the food bank unthinkable.

At 4:00 A.M., with the help of a taxi driver named Mohammed, Dave found an open store. There was one turkey left: twelve pounds, frozen tight, grade B—whatever that meant. It looked like a flesh-coloured bowling ball.

When he took it to the counter, the clerk stared at it in confusion.

"What is that?"said the clerk suspiciously.

"It's a turkey," said Dave.

The clerk shook his head. "Whatever you say, buddy."

As Dave left the store, the clerk called after him, "You aren't going to eat that are you?"

H e was home by 4:30. The first thing he did was make another pot of coffee. Then he went to work on the bird. By 6:30 he had the turkey more or less thawed. He used an electric blanket and a hair dryer.

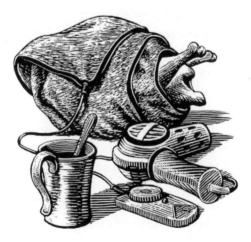

As the turkey defrosted, it became clear what grade B meant. The skin on its right drumstick was ripped. Dave's turkey looked as if it had made a break from the slaughterhouse and dragged itself a block or two before it was captured and beaten to death. Dave began to refer to his bird as Butch. He turned Butch over and found another slash in the carcass. Perhaps, he thought, Butch died in a knife fight.

As sunrise hit Dave through the kitchen window, he ran his hand over his beard and reached for the coffee. He squinted in the morning light, his eyes dark and puffy. He would have been happy if disfiguration was the worst thing about his turkey. Would have considered himself blessed. Would have been able to look back on this Christmas with equanimity. Might eventually have been able to laugh about it. The worst thing came later. After lunch. After Morley and the kids left for the food bank.

Before they left, Morley dropped pine oil on some of the living-room lamps.

"When the bulbs heat the oil up," she said, "the house will smell like a forest." Then she said, "Mother's coming. I'm trusting you with this. You have to have the turkey in the oven—"

Dave finished her sentence for her. "By 1:30," he said. "Don't worry. I know what I'm doing."

The worst thing began when Dave tried to turn on the oven. Morley had never had cause to explain the automatic timer to him, and Dave had never had cause to ask about it. The oven had been set the day before to go on at 5:30. Morley had been baking a squash casserole for Christmas dinner—she always did the vegetables the day before—and now, until the oven timer was unset, nothing anybody did was going to turn it on.

It was 2:00 P.M., and Dave was operating on caffeine and adrenaline. He poured himself another cup to settle his nerves. His hands had begun to shake. There was a ringing in his ears. He knew he was in trouble.

He had to find an oven that could cook the bird quickly. But every oven he could think of already had a turkey in it. For ten years Dave had been technical director of some of the craziest acts on the rock-and-roll circuit. He wasn't going to fall to pieces over a raw turkey.

Inventors are often unable to explain where their best ideas come from. Dave is not sure where he got his. Maybe he had spent too many years in too many hotel rooms. At 2:30 P.M. he threw back one last coffee and phoned the Plaza Hotel. He was given the front desk.

"Do you cook ... special menus for people with special dietary needs?" he asked.

"We're a first-class hotel in a world-class city, sir. We

can look after any dietary needs."

"If someone brings their own food—because of a special diet—would you cook it for them?"

"Of course, sir."

Dave looked at the turkey. It was propped on a kitchen chair like a naked baby. "Come on, Butch," he said, stuffing it into a plastic bag. "We're going out."

Morley had the car. Dave called a taxi. "The Plaza," he said. "It's an emergency."

When Dave arrived in the hotel lobby, the man at the front desk asked if he needed help with his suitcases.

"No suitcases," said Dave, patting the turkey, which he had dropped on the counter and which was now dripping juice onto the hotel floor. Dave turned woozily to the man behind him in line and, slurring slightly, said, "Just checking in for the afternoon with my chick."

The clerk winced. Dave wobbled. He spun around and grinned at the clerk and then around again and squinted at the man in line behind him. He was looking for approval. He found, instead, his neighbour Jim Scoffield. Jim was standing beside an elderly woman whom Dave assumed must be Jim's visiting mother.

Jim didn't say anything, tried in fact to look away. But he was too late. Their eyes had met.

Dave straightened and said, "Turkey and the kids are at the food bank. I brought Morley here so they could cook her for me."

"Oh," said Jim.

"I mean the turkey," said Dave.

"Uh huh," said Jim.

"I bring it here *every* year. I'm alone."

Dave held his arms out as if he were inviting Jim to frisk him.

The man at the desk said, "Excuse me, sir," and handed Dave his key. Dave smiled. At the man behind the counter. At Jim. At Jim's mom. He walked towards the elevators one careful foot in front of the other.

When he got to the polished brass elevator doors, he heard Jim calling him.

"You forgot your ... chick," said Jim, pointing to the turkey Dave had left behind on the counter.

T he man on the phone from room service said, "We have turkey on the *menu, sir.*"

Dave said, "This is ... uh ... a *special* turkey. I was hoping you could cook *my* turkey."

The man from room service told Dave the manager would call. Dave looked at his watch.

When the phone rang, Dave knew this was his last chance. His only chance. The manager would either agree to cook the turkey or he might as well book the ticket to Newfoundland.

"Excuse me, sir?" said the manager.

"I said I need to eat this *particular* turkey," said Dave.

"That *particular* turkey, sir." The manager was non-committal.

"Do you know," said Dave, "what they feed turkeys today?"

"No, sir?" said the manager. He said it like a question.

"They feed them ..."

Dave wasn't at all sure himself. Wasn't so sure where he was going with this. He just knew that he had to keep talking.

"They feed them chemicals," he said, "and antibiotics and steroids and … lard to make them juicier … and starch to make them crispy. I'm allergic to … steroids. If I eat that stuff I'll have a heart attack or at least a seizure. In the lobby of your hotel. Do you want that to happen?"

The man on the phone didn't say anything. Dave kept going.

"I have my own turkey here. I raised this turkey myself. I butchered it myself. This morning. The only thing it has eaten …" Dave looked frantically around the room. What did he feed the turkey?

"Tofu," he said triumphantly.

"Tofu, sir?" said the manager.

"And yoghurt," said Dave.

It was all or nothing.

The bellboy took the turkey, and the twenty-dollar bill Dave handed him, without blinking an eye.

Dave said, "You have those big convection ovens. I have to have it back before 5:30 P.M."

"You must be very hungry, sir," was all he said.

Dave collapsed onto the bed. He didn't move until the phone rang half an hour later. It was the hotel manager.

He said the turkey was in the oven. Then he said, "You raised the bird yourself?" It was a question.

Dave said yes.

There was a pause. The manager said, "The chef says the turkey looks like it was abused."

Dave said, "Ask the chef if he has ever killed a turkey. Tell him the bird was a fighter. Tell him to stitch it up."

T he bellboy wheeled the turkey into Dave's room at quarter to six. They had it on a dolly covered with a silver dome. Dave removed the dome and gasped.

It didn't look like any bird he could have cooked. There were frilly paper armbands on both drumsticks, a glazed partridge made of red peppers on the breast, and a small silver gravy boat with steam wafting from it.

Dave looked at his watch and ripped the paper armbands off and scooped the red pepper partridge into his mouth. He realized the bellboy was watching him and then saw the security guard standing in the corridor. The security guard was holding a carving knife. They obviously weren't about to trust Dave with a weapon.

"Would you like us to carve it, sir?"

"Just get me a taxi," said Dave.

"What?" said the guard.

"I can't eat this here," said Dave. "I have to eat it ..." Dave couldn't imagine where he had to eat it. "Outside," he said. "I have to eat it outside."

He gave the bellboy another twenty-dollar bill and said, "I am going downstairs to check out. Bring the bird and call me a taxi." He walked by the security guard without looking at him.

"Careful with that knife," he said.

Dave got home at 6:00. He put Butch on the table. The family was due back any minute. He poured himself a drink and sat down in the living room. The house looked beautiful—smelled beautiful—like a pine forest.

"My forest," said Dave. Then he said, "Uh oh," and jumped up. He got a ladle of the turkey gravy, and he ran around the house smearing it on light bulbs. There, he thought. He went outside and stood on the stoop and counted to twenty-five. Then he went back in and breathed deeply. The house smelled like ... like Christmas.

He looked out the window. Morley was coming up the walk ... with Jim Scoffield and his mother.

"We met them outside. I invited them in for a drink."

"Oh. Great," said Dave. "I'll get the drinks."

Dave went to the kitchen then came back to see Jim sitting on the couch under the tall swinging lamp, a drop of gravy glistening on his balding forehead. Dave watched another drop fall. Saw the puzzled look cross Jim's face as he reached up, wiped his forehead and brought his fingers

21

to his nose. Morley and Jim's mother had not noticed anything yet. Dave saw another drop about to fall. Thought, Any moment now the Humane Society is going to knock on the door. Sent by the hotel.

He took a long swig of his drink and placed his glass by Morley's hand-painted paper napkins.

"Morley, could you come here?" he said softly. "There's something I have to tell you."